World of Reading

D0010114

+ FUN FACTS

Disney
MICKEY
& FRIENDS

VOTE FOR MINNIE

By **BROOKE VITALE**
Illustrated by the **DISNEY STORYBOOK ART TEAM**

First Paperback Edition, January 2020
1 3 5 7 9 10 8 6 4 2
ISBN 978-1-368-04849-1
FAC-029261-19326
Library of Congress Control Number: 2019910090
Manufactured in the United States of America
For more Disney Press fun, visit www.disneybooks.com

SUSTAINABLE
FORESTRY
INITIATIVE
Certified Sourcing
www.sfiprogram.org
SFI-01415

Disney PRESS
Los Angeles • New York

Mickey, Minnie, and their friends are hiking with the Adventure Club. The club's president, Ludwig von Drake, leads the way.

**THE LEADER OF A CLUB
IS CALLED THE PRESIDENT.**

"Look!" Minnie says. She points at a mountain in the distance. "We should climb Mount Steepness for our next adventure."

"Great idea, Minnie," Ludwig says. "But that will be up to the next club president."

"Next president?" Minnie asks.

Ludwig nods. "Being president is hard work. It's time for someone new to lead the club."

"I'll be the president," Pete says.
He turns to the other club members.
"I'm in charge now!" he shouts.

"Not so fast, Pete," Ludwig says. "Someone else might want to be president. We need to have an election."

"You should run for president, Minnie!" says Mickey. "You would make a great candidate."

Minnie likes that idea. "How does an election work?" she asks. Ludwig says, "First, you have to get your name on the ballot."

"How do we do that?" Pete asks.
"Twenty club members need to sign
your petition," Ludwig says.
"Then you need to raise awareness
and come up with a platform."

The next day, Minnie stands
outside the Adventure Club.
Goofy walks by. "Whatcha doing,
Minnie?" he says.
"I'm collecting signatures,"
Minnie says.

"Gawrsh, that's a funny thing to collect," Goofy says. "I'll stick with my rubber band collection."

THE WORLD'S BIGGEST RUBBER BAND BALL USED 700,000 BANDS AND WEIGHED OVER 9,000 POUNDS!

"It's not that kind of collection, Goofy," Minnie says. "I need twenty signatures on my petition to run for club president."

"Well, why didn't you say so?"
Goofy asks.
Goofy signs Minnie's petition.
Then he signs it again. And again.
"There ya go, Minnie," he says.

Minnie gets twenty *different* signatures. She is on the ballot! But people won't vote for her if they don't know she's running. Minnie needs to raise awareness.

Minnie will ask her friends for help!
On her way to Mickey's house,
she sees Pete.
He is giving away popcorn to raise
awareness.

VOTE FOR PETE

Minnie and her friends come up
with some great ideas to raise
awareness.

Mickey scoops ice cream.
Donald and Daisy hang posters.
Goofy tries to make balloon
animals.

Now Minnie needs to find out what club members want in a leader.

FEMALE SEA TURTLES RETURN TO WHERE THEY WERE BORN TO LAY THEIR EGGS.

The next club event is helping
baby sea turtles to the water.

As Minnie helps, she talks to club
members. She listens to their ideas.

As Mickey and Minnie are leaving the beach, they see Pete building something. "Hiya, Pete," Mickey says. "Whatcha doing?"

"Ludwig said we need to build a platform," Pete says.
Minnie giggles. "I don't think that's the kind of platform Ludwig meant."

The next day, Minnie and Pete
have a debate to talk about
their platforms.
"I will plan safer adventures,
like bird-watching," Pete says.

Minnie thinks club members want more daring adventures. "How about hot-air ballooning, deep-sea diving, or hang gliding?" she says.

THE FIRST HOT-AIR BALLOON FLIGHT WAS IN FRANCE IN 1783. THE BALLOON STAYED IN THE AIR FOR TEN MINUTES.

After the debate, Goofy polls
the audience.
"Everyone I polled is voting
for you!" he tells Minnie.

"That's great!" she says. "Who
did you ask?"
Goofy grins. "Mickey and Daisy."

"Thanks, Goofy," Minnie says. "But I think we need to ask a few more people."

Poll
MINNIE [X] [X]
PETE [ ] [ ]

Soon it is election day. Minnie takes her ballot to a private booth. She fills in the circle next to her name.

Minnie looks around. She is happy
to see so many people voting.

Finally, it is time to count the votes. Pete got twenty-four votes. Minnie got thirty-eight votes. Goofy got one vote!
"Oops," says Goofy. "I thought I was supposed to sign my name!"

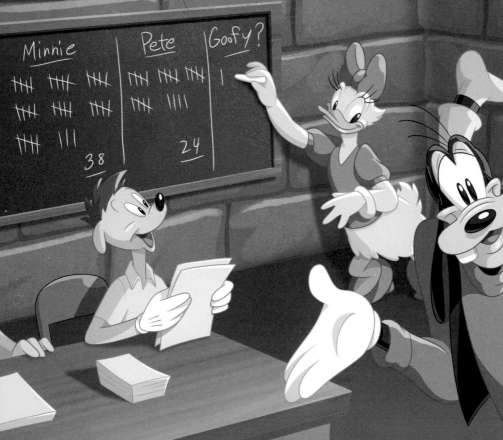

Minnie is the winner!
"Congratulations," Pete says,
shaking Minnie's hand. "You will
be a great president."

A few days later, Minnie
leads the club as they climb
Mount Steepness.
Way to go, President Minnie!